Lost at Sea

Ahoy, mateys!

Set sail for a brand-new
adventure with the

PUPPY PIRATES

PUPPY PIRATES

Lost at Sea

by Erin Soderberg
illustrations by Russ Cox

A STEPPING STONE BOOK™
Random House 🏠 New York

For Russ Cox, whose kindness, generosity,
and talent make him a true inspiration.
I'm so lucky to work with you.
—E.S.

This is a work of fiction. Names, characters, places, and incidents either are the product of the author's imagination or are used fictitiously. Any resemblance to actual persons, living or dead, events, or locales is entirely coincidental.

Text copyright © 2019 by Erin Soderberg Downing and Robin Wasserman
Cover art copyright © 2019 by Luz Tapia
Interior illustrations copyright © 2019 by Russ Cox

Visit us on the Web!
rhcbooks.com

Educators and librarians, for a variety of teaching tools, visit us at
RHTeachersLibrarians.com

Library of Congress Cataloging-in-Publication Data is available upon request.
ISBN 978-0-525-57923-6 (trade) — ISBN 978-0-525-57924-3 (lib. bdg.) —
ISBN 978-0-525-57925-0 (ebook)

Printed in the United States of America
10 9 8 7 6 5 4 3 2 1
First Edition

This book has been officially leveled by using the F&P Text Level Gradient™ Leveling System.

Random House Children's Books supports the First Amendment and celebrates the right to read.

CONTENTS

1

The Legend of the *Grrr*-muda Triangle

"Gather round, pups, for I have a tale to tell." Old Salt rapped his peg leg on the wooden deck of the *Salty Bone*.

A group of puppy pirates trotted over. The Bernese mountain dog was the oldest member of the puppy pirate crew, and he didn't speak often. When he did, everyone listened.

Old Salt cleared his throat. A *whoosh* of sea air ruffled his fur. "Long, long ago in a not-sodistant sea, there was a ship filled with sailors much like you and me."

"Is this a poem?" whined Captain Red Beard. "I don't like poems."

"It's not a poem," Old Salt said. "It's not even a made-up tale. The story I'm about to tell is true."

"Get on with it, then," grumbled Red Beard. The wiry terrier captain was not very patient. He didn't like to wait for much of anything.

"As I was saying—" Old Salt stopped to cough. He coughed and coughed, his whole body shaking. Finally, he opened his mouth wide and coughed out a soggy hair ball. He sighed happily, and then continued his tale. "Long, long ago there was a ship sailing through these very waters. It was a mighty ship, carrying strong, hardworking sailors. This ship was captained by a tough old bulldog, Dread Pirate Wrinkles."

"Is this a story about when you were a pup?" asked Wally, a fluffy golden retriever pup. All the puppies on board the *Salty Bone* longed to know more about Old Salt's past.

Old Salt almost never answered this kind of question. He didn't this time, either. "Dread Pirate Wrinkles's ship carried these sailors through strange, strange waters," he told them. "Into the *Grrr*-muda Triangle. Some call it the Bermuda Triangle. Some call it the Triangle, for short. You young pups ever heard of that?"

Wally shook his head. Many of his mates shook their heads, too. Recess the Labrador retriever, Frosty the husky, the pug twins, and the human boy Henry (Wally's best mate) all looked blankly at Old Salt. Only Millie and Stink, who had spent years living on an old ghost ship, howled "Yes!"

"The Triangle? That's easy!" barked Red Beard. "A triangle is a thing with four sides . . . like a map!"

Wally knew a triangle had *three* sides—and most of their maps were shaped like a *rectangle*. But he didn't want to correct their captain. No one did. Red Beard didn't like to hear when he was wrong.

"Sir," said Curly, the fluffy white mini poodle who served as Red Beard's first mate, "I think Old Salt is talking about the *other* kind of triangle. The mysterious part of the sea where strange things happen. But those are just old legends."

"Are they?" asked Old Salt, a far-off look on his face. "Well, Dread Pirate Wrinkles steered that ship into the Triangle . . . and disappeared. The sails were full. The sea was calm. Everything was going well—until a deep fog blew in from out of nowhere. And—*poof!* Just like that, the ship was gone."

"This Triangle," said Spike, a nervous bull-dog. "Is it . . . *near here?*"

"Aye," woofed Old Salt. "We are sailing toward that part of the sea now."

"What else happens in the *Grrr*-muda Tri-angle?" asked Wally.

Millie woofed, "Pups tell tales of a spooky fog, ripped sails, broken compasses—"

"Weird weather, disappearing supplies . . . that kind of thing," Stink added.

"Don't worry, pups," Curly told the crew. "We are sailing *around* the famous Triangle— not through it. That's the captain's idea." She sniffed. "If you ask me, all these silly stories are nonsense."

"I wouldn't be so sure of that," Old Salt said gruffly.

"Nonsense," Curly said again.

Spike shivered. He squeezed in between Henry and Wally. "Best not to risk it," he said quietly.

"But how does a ship *know* if it's in or out of the Triangle? There is no land anywhere near here to use as map points," Frosty said. Frosty was new to the *Salty Bone* crew. He grew up at the North Pole, where there were always plenty of snow-covered mountains and rivers to use as guides. "So isn't it just a guess?"

"There is a bit of guesswork, yes," answered Curly. "But we have good maps. And, of course, we use nautical map navigation to chart our course."

"Not a *who*-sical navigation?" Captain Red Beard barked. "What kind of hoodly-toodly nonsense are you talking about?"

"I am talking about how we use a compass and maps to figure out our ship's position in the sea," Curly said.

"As I'm sure you already know, Captain," said Einstein, "*nautical* is a fancy word for 'the sea.'"

"Frosty, we use maps, compasses, and islands we have sailed past to track our position from the steering cabin," Curly explained patiently. "We also use the location of the stars at night. All of those tools help us figure out where we are in relation to the Triangle."

"Aye," Old Salt said, tapping his peg leg on

the deck. "But compasses don't always work. They are known to go wonky in the Triangle. And as I always say: if you can't figure out which direction you are pointed in, you can't figure out how to get to where you need to be."

Old Salt was usually the one who calmed all the other pups down. But today there was a look on Old Salt's face that Wally had never seen before. It was a little bit sad, a little bit worried, and maybe even a little bit . . . scared?

No, Wally thought quickly. That couldn't be right. Nothing scared Old Salt. *Nothing.*

Curly barked sharply. "Speaking of *where you need to be* . . ."

Wally knew what that meant. Their story break was over. It was time for afternoon chores! The crew scattered. Steak-Eye made his way down to the kitchen to prepare his famous stew. Henry began to scrub the decks. Wally had finished his chores that morning. And he wanted

to know more about the Triangle! He could tell some of the other pups felt the same way.

"What happened to Dread Pirate Wrinkles's ship?" Wally asked. "Did anyone ever find it?"

Old Salt stared out over the deck rail and said softly, "Maybe it's still in the Triangle to this day. Lost. Sailing around in circles . . ."

"You don't really think that's true, do you?" Recess asked nervously.

"Have *you* ever been inside the Triangle, Old Salt?" asked Wally.

"Did you *see* the ship disappear?" Frosty wondered.

Old Salt turned and looked at each of the young pups in turn. "All I will say is this—" But before he could finish his thought, the ship lurched. The boat tilted to one side. The sails tipped down toward the waves. The crew skidded across the deck, yapping and howling.

"It's the Sea Slug!" wailed Spike. "We're all doomed!"

Crazy Compass

The *Salty Bone* settled quickly, gently rocking in the calm sea. The sails filled with warm wind and billowed in the sunny sky.

But as soon as the pups got their footing, the ship lurched again! The whole crew was flung to the other side of the deck.

Then a bell rang. *DONG! DONG! DONG!*

All the puppy pirates went silent. Because everyone knew that signal: it meant there was trouble!

Slowly and carefully, Old Salt, Wally, and the rest of the pups made their way toward the steering cabin to find out what was the matter.

Captain Red Beard was fighting with the ship's huge wheel. "Blimey!" he shouted, pushing it to port. Then *"Arrrf!"* He swung the wheel to starboard, and the ship lurched with him.

"What's happening, Captain?" asked Henry in alarm. The boy peered out to sea. "Are we under attack?"

"Me compass!" Red Beard howled. "It's goin' crazy!"

Wally climbed into the steering cabin. He studied the huge compass their captain used to navigate. Usually, the compass needle pointed due north at all times.

But at that moment, the needle was wiggling and wobbling all around the face of the compass. One second it was pointing north, then it swished to point east, then it spun around to point west. To avoid the Triangle, they had to sail north. So every time the needle moved, the captain spun the steering wheel to follow it. All that crazy steering was making the boat zigzag through the water.

"In case you were wondering? This isn't good," Henry said, studying the compass. "It seems to be broken."

"What happened?" Curly asked. She hopped up onto a stool and studied the tool. "The compass needle is always supposed to point north. It shouldn't be moving around like that."

Spike wailed. "Nooooooo!"

"What's wrong, Spike?" Wally asked.

"Old Salt's story must be true. I bet we sailed into the Triangle!" Spike whined. "Our compass is broken. We are going to be lost at sea forever. We be dooooomed!"

The rest of the crew began yapping and barking nervously. Old Salt stood quietly, gazing out to sea. Wally thought the strong, old pup looked a little worried, but that couldn't be right. He was the calmest, surest pup Wally had ever met.

"We didn't sail into the Triangle," Curly promised. She turned to the rest of the crew and said loudly, "We *won't* be lost at sea forever. Even if we *had* sailed into the Triangle, there's no truth to all those silly stories. There's just something funny going on with our compass."

"I don't think it's funny," Captain Red Beard

growled. He tugged the wheel left, and the ship lurched again. "Not funny at all."

That's when Wally heard someone giggling on the main deck. *Something funny,* Wally thought. Suddenly, he had a hunch there *was* something funny going on. And it had nothing to do with the magic of the Triangle. He was pretty sure it was a pair of pugs playing a prank. Quietly, Wally jumped out of the steering cabin and poked his nose around a corner.

"Piggly!" he barked, spotting one of the wrinkled pug pups hiding behind a wooden crate. "Puggly! Avast!"

The pug twins snapped to attention. Each sister was holding a string in her mouth. They were both trying to hide giggles. But neither pug was having much luck. The two naughty pranksters liked making mischief almost as much as they liked snacks.

"Did you break the captain's compass?" Wally asked. Pranks were one thing, but breaking stuff was not okay.

"Aw, we didn't break anything, Wally. Just having some fun," Piggly said, her gold tooth glinting. "After hearing Old Salt's story about the Triangle, we thought it would be exciting to spook the crew a little bit."

"Check it out," Puggly said, calling Wally over. "We tied a magnet to a couple of strings. Then we hid the magnet under the compass.

Every time one of us tugs the string, the magnet wiggles, and the compass needle follows it."

"So the compass is not broken?" Wally asked. By now a few of the other pups had gathered around.

"Nope, not broken," Piggly said. "The magnet just messes with it. The compass thinks north is wherever the magnet is. No magnet, no problem. Pirate's promise."

Word about the pugs' prank spread quickly. The whole crew wanted the pugs to show them how the trick worked. Captain Red Beard laughed the whole thing off, pretending he hadn't been fooled by the pugs' silly tricks.

Once he realized what was going on, Spike giggled, too. "I wasn't really that nervous," he lied. "The Triangle is just an old story. Nothing to *really* be scared of." He glanced at Wally and whispered, "Right?"

Wally laughed. "Right. There's no such thing as disappearing ships."

The crew scattered while the captain and Curly got the *Salty Bone* back on course. Wally and Henry stood together, looking out to sea.

"In case you were wondering," Henry said quietly, "that's the famous Triangle, right out there." He gently patted the top of Wally's head.

"We are passing by the Triangle now?" Wally asked, feeling a tingle of nerves race through his legs. "I thought it would be dark and gloomy, or filled with fog or something. . . ."

"The Triangle is just a patch of plain old sea that looks exactly like the rest of the ocean," Henry said. "It's kind of funny, isn't it? That sailors get so worried about a silly old legend."

Wally woofed his agreement. He blinked as a bright flash of sunlight hit him square in the face.

"Did you see that?" Henry asked, shielding his eyes with one hand.

Wally blinked again at another flash of light. Sometimes the sun hit the water just so, making it sparkle. Wally thought it looked like there were pieces of bright, shiny gold floating on the tips of the waves. A moment later, another bright flash.

Then another.

And another.

Wally cocked his head. Three short flashes, three long flashes, then three short flashes again. These flashes didn't look like sparkling sunlight on the sea. They almost seemed like some sort of signal.

"Old Salt!" Wally cried. The old Bernese mountain dog hobbled over to stand at the rail beside him and Henry. "There's something bright inside the Triangle. I don't think it's sunlight." He squinted as the light flashed in his face again. "Is it some sort of signal?"

Old Salt stared into the Triangle. The bright flashes came again—three short, three long, then three short. "Shiver me timbers, lad!" Old Salt barked in alarm. "There's someone calling to us from inside the Triangle! That signal? It's an SOS!"

Save Our Ship!

"An SOS!" Henry shouted to the crew. "Someone inside the Triangle needs our help!"

All the puppy pirates raced over to the ship's port-side rail, waiting for more flashes of light. For several long moments, nothing happened. Then the flashing lights started up again.

Three short flashes.

Three long.

Three short.

"There it is!" Henry shouted, pointing.

"Three dots. Three dashes. Three dots. Which is Morse code for the SOS distress signal."

"What does that mean?" asked Recess.

Old Salt rapped his peg leg on the deck to get the crew's attention. "If someone is in distress, it means they're in trouble."

"But how do you know?" Wally asked. "It's just a bunch of flashing lights."

"Your human is right," Old Salt said. "It's Morse code. That's a way to talk to ships that are very far away. It's a language made out of dots and dashes. A short flash is a dot. A long flash is a dash."

"In case you were wondering, every letter and every number has its own Morse code pattern," Henry said. "The letter *S* is three dots. The letter *O* is three dashes."

"So it's a way to talk without talking?" asked Frosty.

"You could say that," Old Salt agreed. He

heaved a sigh. "And right now it's saying that somewhere inside the Triangle, someone is in trouble. That's what SOS means. *Help*."

"Do you think someone is lost at sea?" Spike asked, his voice shaking with fear.

The flashes of light continued.

• • • /— — —/ • • •
• • • /— — —/ • • •
• • • /— — —/ • • •

Over and over again, the signal came.

"How are they doin' that?" Captain Red Beard asked, scratching his ear. "How are they getting the sun to talk for them?"

"They must be using something shiny to reflect the sunlight," Curly said.

"Something shiny?" Red Beard barked. "Maybe the sun is reflecting off a pile o' gold coins!"

"Are we going to help them?" asked Wally. "We can't just ignore a call for help."

"We'd have to steer off our course . . . ," Curly said, frowning.

In the center of the deck, Einstein laid out a pile of maps. The little wiener dog studied his compass and marked notes on a map. Then he pulled out his spyglass and looked toward the horizon. "Uh, Captain? A word, sir?"

"Speak up," Red Beard ordered. "What is it?"

"If we sail toward the flashing light," Einstein said quietly, "we'll be sailing into the center of the Triangle."

"Nooooooo!" Spike moaned.

"No way," Leo the black Lab said. "You promised we would sail around the Triangle— not through it."

"It sounds dangerous," agreed Wayne the Great Dane.

"Don't be silly!" snarled Curly. "The legend of the Triangle is just that: a *legend*. These are all made-up stories meant to scare pups."

"I'm not so sure of that," said Captain Red Beard. "It does sound scary."

"Nooooooo!" Spike wailed again.

"All of you are being goofy," Curly snipped. "Scared of a bunch of *stories*!"

"Enough!" Old Salt barked, stomping his peg leg. "You are all arguin' about the wrong thing. We shouldn't be talking about whether the Triangle really is dangerous or not. The important question is, are we willing to risk danger in order to rescue those brave sailors?"

"I don't like danger," Spike barked nervously.

"No one likes danger," Old Salt said firmly. "But sometimes we have to face it anyway. Those sailors out there are asking for our help. We have to give it to them. It's the code of the sea."

Wally considered Old Salt's words: *the code of the sea*. What did that mean? Wally wasn't sure. But he *was* sure that Old Salt was right about one thing. If he or any of his friends were in trouble, he would want someone to help. If everyone turned their back on those who needed help, the world would be a much scarier place. The rest of the crew was nodding. Wally could tell that his friends all thought the same thing: like it or not, they had to sail straight into danger.

But it was Captain Red Beard's decision. The

crew waited to see what he would say.

"I think . . ." The captain scratched his beard. He looked at Einstein's maps, then out to sea. He scratched his beard again. When the captain thought, he thought *hard*. Finally, he gave his decision. "Old Salt is right," Red Beard said with a brisk nod of his head. "Puppy pirates must be brave. We're sailing into the Triangle!"

Fog Monster

Wally held his breath as the ship turned slowly toward the Triangle. He couldn't believe they were going to find out what was inside.

"Here we go," Einstein whispered. "If I'm reading my maps correctly, we are passing into the Triangle . . . right *now*!"

As soon as Einstein said the word *now*, Wally felt a blast of cool air hit him square in the face. He shivered, waiting for something horrible to happen. He held his breath.

And waited.

And waited.

But the ship carried on, easily cutting through the deep blue waters.

Wally let out his breath. Maybe all those stories were a bunch of silly nonsense. Surely there was nothing special about this patch of sea. He couldn't believe he had been so worried about sailing into the Triangle.

Turning away from the sea, Wally raced across the deck. It was time for him to take his turn in the crow's nest. Long ago, Wally was scared to go onto the little platform that was used as the ship's lookout. But now he loved climbing up to keep watch. He felt like a bird when he was perched so high in the sky.

Wally raced up the rope ladder. He had just settled in on the wooden platform when thunder boomed. It sounded close. The strange thing was, the skies were sunny and cloudless.

But all sailors knew that sound well. Thunder was a warning of stormy skies and a rough sea. "Storms ahead!" Wally cried.

The thunder echoed and cracked around them. Still, Wally couldn't see any clouds for miles. He was stumped. Suddenly, a wave of fog flowed over the *Salty Bone*'s rails. The thick mist rolled in out of nowhere, covering the ship completely.

In the crow's nest, Wally felt like he was sitting on top of a cloud. The whole ship below him was wrapped in the soupy fog. But the crow's nest was sticking up into clear blue skies. Wally gazed down from his lookout. The fog was so dense that he couldn't even see the pups moving about on the deck! He felt very alone and very far away.

The foghorn sounded from inside the steering cabin.

Toooot!

Toooot!

Toooot!

Wally could hear the captain shouting orders. The puppy pirates had sailed through fog before, of course, but it had never been like this! Wally knew his role as lookout pup was more important than ever. Captain Red Beard would need him to keep his eyes open for other ships or obstacles in the sea ahead of them.

Fixing his sights past the ship's bow, Wally noticed something strange. The fog was *only* around their ship. The rest of the Triangle was sunny. "Clear skies in view!" he called to his mates below.

But almost as soon as he said that, Wally spotted something else. Another patch of fog had formed. It hung low over another part of the water. As Wally watched, the fog grew and shifted. It almost looked as if the fog was turning into giant tentacles, snaking out of the water. The fog arms reached for the *Salty Bone,* curling and bending as they got closer, closer. . . .

Wally gulped and closed his eyes tight. "Avast!" he cried. Maybe all the stories about the Triangle weren't so crazy after all! "FOG MONSTER!" he howled. Wally felt a little silly yelling something so strange. But he had to make sure the crew was ready for whatever might be sneaking up on them.

"The Triangle is attacking us!" Spike wailed. His voice was loud enough that Wally could hear him easily. "Thunder, fog, now a *monster?* It's telling us not to go any farther."

"Enough nonsense," Curly yipped. "It's just fog and some stray thunder. There's no such thing as fog monsters. Stop letting your eyes play tricks on you, Wally!"

Wally opened his eyes. The fog was gone. Their ship was sailing through bright, clear, sparkling seas again. He was embarrassed. *Had* he let his eyes play tricks on him? No, Wally was pretty sure of what he had seen. The fog *had* looked like a monster. But then Wally thought about how the clouds sometimes looked like animals, too. He was letting Old Salt's tale get the best of him.

Moments later, a horrible sound rang out from somewhere nearby: *Yeeee-ow!*

The hair on Wally's neck lifted. The thunder was scary. The fog had been spooky. But this sound? It was even worse.

The screeching yowls echoed all around them. *Yeeee-ow! Yeeee-ow! Yeeee-ow!*

Wally spotted a small lifeboat straight ahead on the horizon. The boat was flashing the SOS signal. These were the sailors they had come to save! The puppy pirates all gave a cheer. They had done it! They had saved the day! Wally felt very proud of himself. Sometimes it was fun to be brave.

The *Salty Bone* sailed closer and closer to the stranded sailors. Soon they would be near enough to pull them onto the ship. But there was something strange about the lifeboat. Wally peered down at the creatures inside it. They almost looked like—

"Is that," Captain Red Beard howled, "a CAT?"

Pause for Claws

"What in the name of Growlin' Grace is *that*?" Captain Red Beard barked. "I must be seein' things, because that sure looks like a boat full o' stinky kitten pirates. Tell me I'm seein' things!"

No one could tell him that. Because there was no doubt about it. The boat bobbing on the waves was full of cats.

The puppy pirates and the kitten pirates had been enemies for as long as anyone could remember. Their two ships had crossed paths

many times while they were racing for the same treasure, battling each other, or hunting the famous Sea Slug. Once, Wally and a few of his mates were taken prisoner on the kitten pirates' ship, the *Nine Lives*. That was a day he would never forget.

Wally raced down from the crow's nest to join the others. They had to talk about what they were going to do. As the lifeboat drew closer, Wally spotted Moopsy and Boopsy, the naughty Siamese cats. Fluffy the Claw, the kitten pirates' first mate, stood at the bow. All the cats bobbing in the little boat looked wet and skinny and a little scared.

Wally could see that there was also a girl sitting in the middle of the small, crowded lifeboat. A tiny gray kitten was perched on her shoulder. The girl was Ruby, the only human who lived on the kitten ship. The kitten was Ruby's best mate, Pete the Mighty. The girl was wearing a big, round, shiny necklace. That's what the kittens were using to reflect the sun and send out their SOS signals.

"Shiver me timbers," Henry cried. "Is that you, Ruby?"

The girl scowled back. "Aye. It's me."

Henry waved. "Looks like you and your mates could use some help."

Ruby crossed her arms over her chest. "We don't want any help from the likes of you."

A chorus of hissing and howls rang out from the lifeboat. "We can't afford to be picky!" one cat hissed.

"But they're *dogs*!" Fluffy the Claw screeched.

"We won't survive out here much longer," a soft voice argued.

On the puppy pirate ship, Captain Red Beard was fuming. "This is an outrage!" he barked. "We risked our lives to sail into the Triangle for a bunch of *kittens*?"

"Sir," Spike said, his voice shaking, "do you think this could be some sort of trap?"

"A trap?" Red Beard howled. He stomped his paw on the deck. "Of course it's a trap. Those furry scalawags *tricked* us into sailing into the Triangle. Now they're probably going to try to sneak on board our ship and steal all me loot!"

"I'm not so sure about that," Curly said. "How could this be a trap? The kitten pirates had no way of knowing the *Salty Bone* would be sailing by. If you ask me, these cats look like they're in real trouble."

"That's one wet pile of kittens," Henry added. "Don't look so fierce when they're all soaked with water, do they?"

"Henry has a point," Wally said. "They don't look very fierce."

"How much of a threat could a handful of soggy cats really be?" Curly asked.

"Are you sayin' you want me to *invite* our enemy to board this ship?" Red Beard howled.

Curly cocked her head. "We can't just leave them out here."

The rest of the crew grumbled their agreement.

Captain Red Beard shook his head. "Unbelievable. I've got a crew full of softies." He leaned over the ship's rail and shouted, "What are you doing out here in the Triangle, kitten pirates? And what am I supposed to do about it?"

"Are you going to help us or not?" Ruby snapped.

"How did you end up stranded in that junky little lifeboat?" Henry asked.

The puppy pirate crew watched with great interest as Henry and Ruby stared each other down.

Ruby put her hands on her hips and glared at Wally's best mate. "The story of how we got here is none of your business."

"Okay, then," Henry said, waving. "See ya! Good luck out there!"

"Wait!" Moopsy the Siamese cat cried. "I'll tell you."

All the pups hung over the edge of the deck, waiting. Moopsy went on, "We were sent on a special mission by our captain. Lucinda the Loud heard a story about an old ship that disappeared in the Triangle long ago. The ship was filled with hardworking sailors traveling to far-off places. That ship's captain was the legendary Dread Pirate Wrinkles. We are on a quest to find his ship, to see if we can find its treasure."

Wally exchanged nervous looks with some of the other puppy pirates. This sounded an awful lot like Old Salt's story.

Boopsy took over for her sister. "But as we rowed through the Triangle in this lifeboat, we were hit by a storm and lost our oars. We have been stranded ever since. We were starting to lose all hope."

"You're not really going to ditch us here, are you?" Ruby asked.

"Just admit that you need our help!" Henry shouted.

Ruby looked furious. But she also looked like someone with no other choice.

"We need to get back to our ship," she finally admitted. "It's waiting for us on Clawfish Island. That is just outside the Triangle. Will you take us?"

Captain Red Beard and Curly talked it over

quietly. It was agreed. They would drag the boatload of kittens and their human onto the *Salty Bone*.

The kitten pirates tried to paddle toward the puppy pirate ship. But since none of the cats wanted to get their claws wet, it was a long process. Finally, Red Beard grew impatient and tossed the kittens a rope.

Ruby tugged.

Henry tugged.

Ruby tugged harder.

Henry tugged even *harder*.

Finally, the little lifeboat clunked against the side of the *Salty Bone*. The kitten pirates climbed on board. They stared in wonder.

"Well, shiver me timbers," Fluffy the Claw whispered. "I never thought I would set paw on the *Salty Bone*."

For a few moments, the two crews stared each other down. Finally, Red Beard ordered his crew to set a course to sail out of the Triangle as quickly as possible. "Let's get rid of these cats

as fast as we can," the captain barked, "and never set paw or tail in this creepy Triangle again!"

The ship cut through the water, zooming toward Clawfish Island. "In case you were wondering," Henry announced loudly, "if we catch the winds just right, we should be safely out of the Triangle in less than half an hour."

Behind him, Ruby shivered. "Good. I don't usually believe silly old legends. But I've got to admit, the Triangle gives me the creeps. I don't like this place at all."

Just as Ruby said that, another loud clap of thunder boomed overhead. The sun dipped behind a wall of low clouds. Lightning streaked the sky. Wind tore at the *Salty Bone*'s sails. Rain poured down.

"I don't think the Triangle likes you very much, either," Henry said, grinning.

Then, just as suddenly as it had come, the rain stopped. Around them, the sky was now green and murky. The wind died down and the ship's sails sagged.

"This feels like the eye of a hurricane," Ruby whispered. "It's eerie."

The ship bobbed calmly on the sea. "In case anyone was wondering? We're not going anywhere," Henry announced. "The wind is *gone*."

"Is it just me," Spike whimpered, "or does it almost seem like now that we're here, the Triangle doesn't *want* us to leave?"

Stranger Things

"I blame this on you!" Captain Red Beard growled at the pack of cats.

"Us?" hissed Fluffy the Claw. He and the rest of the kitten pirates were huddled together, licking their paws and trying to get warm under a pile of blankets. "How can you blame us for the weather?"

"He has a point," Curly said. "Cats can't do much—"

"Hey!" Boopsy yelped, cutting her off. "Anything dogs can do, cats can do better!"

"Pups can do *everything* better than you," Red Beard snapped back.

"No, you can't," Moopsy said.

"Yes, we can!" Red Beard woofed.

Old Salt cleared his throat loudly. "Last time I checked, neither cats *nor* dogs can control the weather."

"Exactly!" Curly yipped. "There's no one to blame for this. It's just bad luck."

"Looks like we have no choice," Henry said. "We'll have to wait out the storm."

Spike whined and hid his face in his paws. "We're never going to get out of here," he panted. "We're going to be stuck in the Triangle forever. Is our ship going to disappear?" He raced to the port-side rail and looked down into the water. "If our ship disappears, we'll all fall into the sea. I don't know how to swim and I'm going to sink and then the Fog Monster will get me and—"

"Enough!" Curly snapped. "There is no sense getting yourself worked up. It's just unusual weather. It will pass."

Millie and Stink offered to sing a few songs to help pass the time. Einstein studied his maps. Captain Red Beard worked with a few of the larger pups to adjust the sails to see if they could catch even a little gust of wind.

As soon as everyone was busy, the pugs trotted over to Wally. *"Psst,"* Piggly said with a naughty gleam in her eye. "Wally!"

"Aye?" Wally said.

"Snack time!" Puggly told him.

Wally loved the sound of that. He tugged at Henry's shirt. Then the two friends followed the pugs down the stairs to the ship's galley. They snuck past the ship's cook, Steak-Eye, who was growling about having to feed a bunch of cats. They made their way past bubbling pots of stew. The pugs led them toward the crates of treats hidden in a back corner of the galley. "Yummy yummy yummy," Piggly said, her tongue lolling out of her mouth.

She was just about to nose open a crate when a voice bellowed, "Are you sneaking food?"

Henry and the three pups whipped around. Ruby stood behind them, her arms folded across her chest. Pete the Mighty was perched on her shoulder, like a parrot.

"It's none of your business," Henry snapped, putting his finger to his lips. "And keep your voice down."

"It sure *is* my business," Ruby said quietly. "My mates and I have been stuck in a lifeboat without food for days. If you've got food, we want some."

Henry sighed. "Fine. Keep a lookout for Steak-Eye, and we'll share with you."

The pugs nudged the crate of treats open. "It's empty!" Piggly wailed.

Puggly pawed open another crate. "This one is empty, too!"

Henry peered into a third crate. "In case you were wondering, they're all empty!"

Ruby took a deep breath. She shook her head. "The Triangle strikes again," she said.

"The Triangle?" Wally and the pugs yelped at the same time.

"What does the Triangle have to do with this?" Henry asked.

"Missing food, strange storms, no wind . . . ,"

Ruby said in a hush. "It's all part of the legend. All we need now is a bunch of fog, some ripped sails, and a broken compass . . . and we're doomed."

"We sailed through fog," Henry admitted. "When we were following your SOS signal. It got very foggy all of a sudden. The ship was totally covered in fog."

"Uh-oh," Ruby said. "That's not good."

Then a voice rang out from the main deck. "Captain!" one of the deckhands barked. "There's a rip in the main sail."

Ruby and Henry looked at each other. The pugs hopped into the empty crates. Wally's tail drooped.

Ruby's eyes went wide with fear. "This is not good at all."

The Tail End of
Old Salt's Tale

Wally and his friends raced out of the kitchen. Ruby chased after Henry and the others as they ran up the stairs. She cuddled her kitten mate safely inside her arms. The group slid across the deck just as Leo and some of the other deckhands dropped a shredded sail on the ship's deck.

"Well, shiver me timbers," grumbled Captain Red Beard. "It must have ripped in the wind."

"Could be that," Spike said. The chubby bulldog was trembling. "Or it could be that the legend of the Triangle is coming true. First there was the fog, then that weird storm, now we have a ripped sail—"

"And our food is gone!" Piggly barked loudly. "The treats? They disappeared!"

All the puppy pirates began barking at once. The kitten pirates meowed and wailed.

"We're doomed!" shrieked Moopsy.

"The Triangle is trying to eat us!" hissed Boopsy.

"I need a hug and a cuddle!" wailed Fluffy the Claw.

"Avast! Stop being such a pack of scaredy-cats," Curly ordered. "There has to be a good explanation for all of this nonsense."

Maybe there was, maybe there wasn't. Recess, Frosty, and a few of the youngest pups looked very scared. Spike was hiding under his favorite blanket. Einstein had buried himself under a pile of crumpled maps.

Wally tried to keep his tail up. He knew it was important to be brave and strong to help his mates . . . even if he would rather snuggle tight inside his bunk and hide with Henry.

"Captain!" Wayne called from the steering cabin. "Captain, you need to come quickly."

The whole pack followed as Captain Red Beard trotted toward the steering cabin. "What is it?" he asked.

"The compass, sir," said Wayne. "It's—it's broken. Again."

Wally looked at the pugs. So did many of the other puppy pirates. But both of the naughty pugs shook their heads. "It wasn't us this time," Puggly promised. "We were in the galley."

"You say it's broken?" Red Beard asked, scratching his head. "Are you sure?"

Wayne howled. "*Aye, aye arrrr-oooo!* I'm sure. How will we steer our way out of the Triangle if we don't know where we're going?"

Curly pushed through the pack and stormed into the steering cabin. "Impossible," she said. "Someone must be playing tricks on us. Someone like . . ."

The tough-talking first mate glared at the kitten pirates. They were all squished together, looking like a messy pile of fur with many heads.

"Someone like a *cat*. That sail could easily have been ripped by one of *your* filthy claws. Are you also responsible for this broken compass? Did you *steal* our food?"

The puppy pirates growled and snarled at the cats.

The kitten pirates showed their claws. They arched their backs.

"It was you, eh?" Captain Red Beard snapped. "You think you can play tricks on us, do ya? If you mess with us, we'll send you back to your lifeboat, and you can fend for yourselves."

The kitten pirates weren't going to take the blame without fighting back. "You can't blame us for your broken-down boat!" Fluffy the Claw said.

"Blame the Triangle!" said Moopsy.

"It's trying to trap us all," agreed Boopsy.

"We never should have brought you stinky furballs on board our ship," Red Beard said.

"Cats can never be trusted."

"All of you, hush," Old Salt barked, rapping his peg leg on the deck. "Settle in. I'm going to tell you a story."

Curly sighed. "Old Salt, the last thing anyone on this ship needs right now is another scary story. Don't you think we have enough trouble as it is?"

Old Salt coughed up another hair ball. "This story is true," he said, his voice hoarse. "It's the story of how I became a pirate."

There was a murmur of excitement. *That* was a story every pup wanted to hear. Even at a time like this. The cats pretended they weren't listening, but Wally could see them all prick up their ears.

"Many long years ago," Old Salt began, "I was sailing through the Triangle in a ship much like this one. The ship was carrying a load of pups to a wonderful farm that had hired us to help watch over their animals and land."

"You were a farm dog?" Wally asked. He was excited. Wally had lived on a farm before joining the puppy pirate crew!

"I didn't say that," Old Salt told him with a small, mysterious smile. "Besides, that detail is not important to this story. As I was saying, I was on a ship filled with Bernese mates and many other types of pups—all of whom were going off on adventures of their own. The ship we were traveling on was captained by . . . Dread Pirate Wrinkles."

All the puppy pirates gasped.

Old Salt waited for everyone to settle, then continued his story. "We were crossing the Triangle when, suddenly, a storm came out of nowhere. It knocked our ship to and fro. I had never seen a storm like that. In all the tipping and turning, I was knocked overboard. The crew tried to save me. They dropped a lifeboat. But as soon as I got into the little boat, I was blown away from the main ship. I watched my mates disappear into the fog. I was alone in a lifeboat, in the middle of the *Grrr*-muda Triangle."

"So that story of the disappearing ship you told . . . It was *your* ship that disappeared?" Frosty asked, his face filled with wonder.

"Aye," Old Salt said. "It disappeared from view. I was left to save myself."

"What happened?" asked Recess, her eyes wide.

"I floated in that boat for days," Old Salt said. "A few other ships passed near me, but no one stopped. I don't know if they didn't see me . . . or if they chose not to see me. Many of those boats were busy doing their own thing, and they were filled with pups who were very different from me. Some were busy carrying human passengers, hauling supplies, or fishing for food. They were all focused on their own business, and none of them could stop to help a stranger. Until one day, someone did come to my rescue."

"Who?" Red Beard asked.

"It was a pirate ship," said Old Salt. "A pirate ship filled with both dogs *and* cats."

"Puppy pirates *and* kitten pirates?" Wally asked. He was surprised to hear this. He had only known kittens as the enemy. Had dogs and cats once been friends? It must have been a very long time ago.

"Aye," said Old Salt. "And you know what? It was one of the cats who convinced the crew to stop for me. Once they pulled me off that lifeboat, she told me why they had stopped. She said they were following the code of the sea. It didn't matter that I wasn't one of them. It only mattered that I was a pirate at heart. She knew I had pirate blood in me because I had fought to survive in the Triangle. And that made me one of them."

Old Salt gazed around at all his fellow pirates. "That's why no one is leaving anyone anywhere. We're pirates. No matter how different we might look from one another, we all have a little something in common. We're all in this together, and we're going to get out of it together."

Create a Compass

As Old Salt finished his story, a light wind began to blow out of the west. The clouds lifted and the sky cleared.

"I can try to repair this sail so we can get on our way," Ruby said.

"I'll help," offered Henry. "I guess it doesn't matter how it ripped. What matters is that it's fixable."

The two humans got to work mending the sail. Meanwhile, the pugs led a search for the missing snacks. They started by asking Steak-Eye where he saw them last.

"I saw them exactly where I hid them," Steak-Eye said.

"*You* hid the snacks?" Puggly said, confused. "From what?"

"From you two," Steak-Eye said. "And I hid them where you would never find them."

The snacks were in the cleaning closet! The pug twins were always trying to get out of work, so Steak-Eye knew they would never look in there.

No one could explain the strange weather— that was still a mystery. But now that the clouds had cleared, it seemed like smooth sailing from here on out. The only problem? Their compass was still broken.

"Without our compass, we have no idea which way we're sailing," Einstein pointed out. "We can read our maps to see where we need to go, but we might be sailing in the exact wrong direction. If the current is strong enough, we might even sail in circles."

"It will be night soon," Curly said. "We can try to use the North Star to guide us."

Spike shuddered. "I don't want to be in the Triangle at night. Let's get out of here while the sun's still shining!"

"Do you have an idea for how we can fix this compass, then?" Curly asked.

"I do," offered Fluffy the Claw.

All the dogs spun around and stared at the kitten pirate. "You do?" asked Captain Red Beard.

"Aye," Fluffy the Claw said. "There's an old, wise cat who lives on our ship. She taught us how to build our *own* compass. She always says, 'If you can't figure out which direction you are pointed in, you can't figure out how to get to where you need to be.'"

"Old Salt always says that, too!" Wally woofed. He glanced at the old pup and thought the Bernese mountain dog winked at him. But he couldn't be sure.

"So are you going to tell us, or what?" Red Beard barked.

"All we need is a cork, a bowl of water, a metal pin of some kind, and a magnet," Fluffy the Claw said. "With those four simple things, we can make a compass."

Pups scattered, searching for the supplies they needed. Puggly brought a couple of hairpins she used to attach her bows. "Will these work?" she asked. Fluffy the Claw nodded.

Steak-Eye set out a bowl of water. Einstein found a cork in the galley. Piggly galloped across the deck, carrying the pugs' magnet in her mouth.

"I've got it!" Piggly cried. "The final piece!" She raced forward, her little paws pounding on the deck. But just as she drew near, she tripped on the bowl of water. It spilled, sending water everywhere. Piggly's paws slid in four different directions. She skidded across the slippery deck. The magnet flew out of her mouth. Everyone watched in horror as the magnet tumbled through the air—and over the ship's rail. It landed with a *plop!* in the water far below.

"Nooooooo!" wailed Captain Red Beard.

"This is it," howled Spike. "We are going to be lost in the Triangle forever."

"Not so fast," said Old Salt. "I have another idea."

Wally and the other pups pricked up their ears.

Old Salt said, "Many long years ago, a very wise sailor showed me another way to build a compass. We didn't have a magnet. So she showed me how to use *fur* to magnetize the compass instead. We just have to rub our compass needle with a bit of fur, and it should point north."

Captain Red Beard sat on one of Puggly's metal hairpins. He wiggled his rump around. "Like this?"

"Not exactly." Old Salt chuckled. "Any of you kittens want to lend me a tail?"

Moopsy volunteered. Old Salt showed

Henry how to rub the hairpin along the fur, over and over, always in the same direction. "After fifty strokes, it should be magnetized."

The puppies and the kittens counted out loud together, all the way up to fifty.

When the hairpin was ready, Old Salt pushed it into the cork. Finally, he dropped the cork and pin into a fresh bowl of water. Wally held his breath. Would this really work? It seemed like magic.

"It floats!" cried Captain Red Beard. "Look at that!"

The homemade needle slowly spun in the water. Finally, it settled in place, pointing at the starboard side of the ship.

"In case you were wondering," Henry said, peering over the bowl. "A magnetized needle will point north and south." He pointed toward the bow of the ship. "And since the sun is beginning to set in front of us, we must be going west right now."

"So north is that way?" Wally asked, looking over the starboard rail.

"That is correct," said Old Salt. "It looks like it is time for us to be on our way."

A Colorful Goodbye

Captain Red Beard ordered his crew to set their ship's course due east. According to Einstein, this was the quickest path out of the Triangle. "If I am reading my maps correctly," he said, "this route should also take us straight past Clawfish Island."

"Then we can get rid of these filthy kittens and be on our way," Red Beard said joyfully.

The wind was now blowing firmly out of the west, nudging their ship in the right direction.

Wally thought it seemed as if the Triangle was helping to lead their ship to safety—and the kittens back to their crew.

With the day turning quickly into evening, the puppy pirates sang pirate shanties as they raised their sails and set off. The ship bounced merrily on the waves. No more thunder echoed in the sky. The fog was long gone. In some ways, it felt like everything that had happened in the Triangle had been some sort of strange dream.

The sky had shifted to a deep purple color. A full moon lit up the night, casting enough light that it looked as if thousands of diamonds were shimmering on the surface of the water.

Steak-Eye hauled out a feast for everyone. He even offered the kitten pirates some of his famous stew. The cats sniffed it from a distance. At first, they turned up their noses, then turned and flicked their tails at the meal. But the kitten pirates were so hungry that none of them could

act snobby and picky for long. Soon they were lapping up every morsel and begging for more.

"This is the *purr*-fect thing to fill my belly after so many days without food," Boopsy sighed. "Dog food isn't half bad, you know?"

Wally and Steak-Eye exchanged knowing looks. The two of them and Henry were the only sailors on board who knew about Steak-Eye's secret ingredient: kitty food! It was no wonder the cats were enjoying their supper so much.

"Don't get used to this kindness," Captain Red Beard growled at the cats. "Just because our two crews teamed up to save everyone's hides today, it doesn't mean we're mates now."

"Aye," Fluffy the Claw hissed. "Enemies always."

"Always," Red Beard vowed.

"But," Fluffy the Claw added quietly, "if your pack ever finds itself in a mess where you need a few extra paws . . . we do owe you for coming to our rescue. I've heard cats have nine lives. I *might* be willing to spare part of one to help a fellow pirate in need."

Red Beard and Fluffy the Claw shook on the deal.

"This is it, mates," Einstein said suddenly, looking up from his pile of maps. "We are just about to sail out of the Triangle."

"*Arrrr-oooo!*" Spike howled. "*Arrrr-oooo!*"

Old Salt hobbled toward the ship's stern. Wally joined him. Together, the two pups looked out over the waters they had just sailed through. With a nod of his head, Old Salt said, "Farewell, Triangle."

Wally sniffed at the sea air. There was something . . . *strange* in this wind. His fur rose, and his tail stiffened. He felt sure that something was going to happen. But what now?

Suddenly, the sky lit up with a thousand

colors. Scarlet, orange, yellow, teal, and emerald lights streaked across the night sky. The colors danced along the horizon, wiggling and swaying like waves. It almost seemed as if the Triangle was saying goodbye in its own mysterious way.

"What in the name of Growlin' Grace is going on?" barked Captain Red Beard.

"That looks like the northern lights," Henry said, his face filled with wonder.

"Aye," Curly agreed. "But we don't usually see the northern lights this far south. Seeing them in the sky way down in warm waters like this? It just doesn't make sense."

"'Tis another mystery of the *Grrr*-muda Triangle," Old Salt said quietly.

Wally wondered if maybe there was something magical about the Triangle after all. He had a feeling he might not ever know for sure.

10

The Code of the Sea

They sailed east through calm waters. Soon Wally spotted the hulking outline of Clawfish Island in the distance. When they got a little closer, he could also see the *Nine Lives* anchored just offshore. The kitten pirate ship looked a lot like the *Salty Bone* from a distance—but Wally knew it was very different on the inside!

"Home, sweet home," Ruby said, grinning at the kitten ship. Then she yelped in alarm as a hair ball flew straight toward her! Ruby ducked

just in time, and the hair ball landed with a *pluffff* on the deck. Cat hair exploded into the air. More hair-ball missiles followed. The puppy pirates were under attack!

"Ready the water cannons!" Captain Red Beard barked into his megaphone. "Prepare to fire."

"Hold your fire!" Ruby called into the night.

"It's us, Captain!" shouted Boopsy.

"Who is *us*?" screeched the kitten pirate

captain, Lucinda the Loud. "Announce your-self."

"Your missing crew!" Fluffy the Claw shouted back.

"*Fluffy?*" Lucinda the Loud wailed. "*Is that you?* We've been waiting forever for you!"

"Aye," sighed Fluffy the Claw. "'Tis me. The pirate called *Fluffy the Claw.* Also Moopsy, Boopsy, the girl, and—"

Lucinda the Loud interrupted him. "What are you doing on a *puppy* ship?"

"It's a long story," Fluffy the Claw cried. "Permission to board our ship?"

"Who's asking?" she screamed.

Fluffy the Claw sighed again. "It is still I," he said loudly, "your first mate, Fluffy the Claw."

"You may board," the kitten pirate captain called.

The *Salty Bone* drew up beside the *Nine Lives.* The kitten pirates were carefully moved from one ship to the other. Ruby glanced back at Henry as she left. Pete the Mighty meowed at Wally. "Thanks," Ruby said with a shrug. "It doesn't smell half as bad on this ship full of mutts as I would have expected."

As the cats left the *Salty Bone*, Red Beard and Lucinda the Loud stared each other down. It looked like they were both expecting the other to pull a dirty trick. But the two captains honored their agreement, and all the kittens made it safely back to their ship.

Lucinda the Loud stood at the rail of the *Nine Lives*. "*Captain Red Beard,*" she shouted, "to thank you for helping my crew, I would like to offer you a reward: the promise of a temporary truce. We will not attack. Instead, we will allow you to sail away safely."

"You will *allow* us to sail away safely?" Red Beard laughed. "That is not much of a reward. Those are usually shiny or golden or fancy."

Lucinda the Loud nodded. "Fair enough. Lower your sails so that I might send over a small gift to show our appreciation."

The promise of treasure was enough to convince Captain Red Beard. He sat and waited, while Lucinda the Loud and Fluffy the Claw prepared their gift.

A few minutes later, a small group of kitten pirates rowed back over to the *Salty Bone* to deliver the package. In the dinghy were Moopsy,

Boopsy, Ruby, Pete the Mighty, and an old matted cat who looked like she had sailed around the world three hundred times.

Red Beard tore open the gift. Inside was a new compass. It was crusted in rubies and emeralds that shone even in the dim light of the moon. Captain Red Beard sighed happily. "This will do," he said. He licked the compass to claim it as his own. Then he gently carried it in his mouth to the steering cabin.

Before the kitten pirates could return to their ship, Old Salt stopped them. "I think we also owe *you* a thank you," he said. "We couldn't have gotten out of that Triangle without some very good advice." He looked at the old cat and cocked his head.

She flicked her tail at him in response. Her gaze shifted to the homemade compass that was still sitting in the center of the *Salty Bone*'s main deck. "I see you were paying attention to what I taught you," she said, a smile tugging at the corners of her mouth.

Old Salt nodded. Then he lowered his head in a bow. "Aye," he said. "That I did, Snarlin' Sue. It's been a long time, but there is much that I remember from your teachings."

Wally looked from Old Salt to the old cat, Snarlin' Sue. "Is this . . . ," he began. "Is this the cat who rescued you from the Triangle, Old Salt?"

"Were the two of you on a crew together when you were little?" Frosty asked eagerly.

"What happened to your ship?" wondered Spike.

"Do you know anything more about Dread Pirate Wrinkles or the ship that disappeared in the Triangle?" Recess asked Snarlin' Sue.

Snarlin' Sue coughed up a laugh. "Have you

been telling your mates some tall tales?" she asked Old Salt.

Old Salt laughed, too.

It was strange, Wally thought. Even though Old Salt was a dog and Snarlin' Sue was a cat, their laughter sounded exactly the same.

"Ah, they all know you shouldn't believe anything an old pirate has to say!" Old Salt said. He winked at Snarlin' Sue.

She winked back. Then the old cat strutted toward the ladder. "Come along, mates," called Snarlin' Sue to the kittens. With a farewell flick of her tail, she meowed, "There are some adventures that will have to remain our little secret . . . for now."

All paws on deck!

Want another
Puppy Pirates adventure?
Here's a sneak peek at

Catnapped!

It was an ambush! The entire kitten crew was crawling over the hillside. The cats were clearly angry, all hisses and claws. The town pups ran off, but the puppy pirates prepared for a fight.

Most of the puppy pirates, anyway. Not Spike. He just roamed in circles, shaking with terror. "What do we do? What do we *do-oooo-ooooo*?"

Captain Red Beard pushed to the front of his crew. He went nose to nose with the kitten captain. "We had a deal, Captain Lucinda the Loud! We no attacky you, you no attacky us."

Lucinda the Loud hissed. "We *had* a deal . . . until your pugs broke the rules. Bad dogs! You should know better than to play catnip pranks on Moopsy and Boopsy."

"Uh-oh," Piggly squeaked. She and Puggly quickly backed away from the face-off. They ducked beneath a leafy bush.

"Moopsy and Boopsy?" Puggly snorted, once

they were safely out of sight. She tried to hide her giggles inside her cape. "The Siamese cats are named *Moopsy* and *Boopsy*?" Laughing and sneezing, she poked her sister. "Piggly, come with me. I've got an idea!"

No one but Wally noticed the pugs sneak away. All eyes were on the two pirate captains.

"You're outnumbered!" Lucinda the Loud yelled. "You have no choice but to surrender."

"Never!" Red Beard barked. "Puppy pirates, prepare for battle!"

New friends. New adventures.
Find a new series . . . just for you!

ISADORA MOON

ISADORA MOON Goes to School

Harriet Muncaster

For ballerina and fairy and vampire lovers

COMMANDER IN CHEESE

COMMANDER IN CHEESE The Big Move

Lindsey Leavitt illustrated by A. G. Ford

For adventurers

JULIAN'S WORLD
THE STORIES JULIAN TELLS

JULIAN'S WORLD THE STORIES JULIAN TELLS

PUPPY PIRATES

PUPPY PIRATES Stowaway!

Erin Soderberg

For dog lovers

PuRRmaids

PuRRmaids The Scaredy Cat

For mermaid and cat lovers

BALLPARK Mysteries SUPER SPECIAL #1
THE WORLD SERIES CURSE

David A. Kelly

For sports fans

1220a

RHCB RHCBooks.com